The Best Kind of Dad

Story by Melaina Faranda
Illustrations by Nathalie Ortega

Contents

Chapter 1

Snail

Sam felt sick.

Dad stopped washing up the breakfast dishes to sign. He raised two pointed fingers above his head – this meant "snail".

On any other day, this would have been Dad's way of joking. As the fastest kid at his old school, Sam was known for always being first in line and on time. But today, he was going to a new school – a school that hadn't been set up specially for the deaf. Sam's dad was deaf, too, and when he was a boy, he hadn't gone to a deaf school. But then, Sam knew Dad was braver than him.

Sam wished Mum was with them, but she had already flown out to start her new job. It was Dad who now signed how proud he was of Sam for starting this new adventure.

"This is our new student – Sam," Mr Wilson announced to the class. "Sam might be unable to hear me or you speaking out loud, but I'm told he's a champion lip-reader. So, everyone, please always make sure Sam can see you talking."

Mr Wilson sat Sam at a front table so that whenever Mr Wilson spoke, Sam had a direct view of his mouth. Mostly, Sam could lip-read the teacher's instructions, but there was another teacher to show Sam anything he missed.

It was easy for Sam to tell when the bell rang, because the whole class sprang from their seats to stream outside into the playground.

A boy darted over to where Sam sat alone on a bench. "Can you play football?" the boy asked.

Sam nodded.

"Good. You can be on our team. I'm Rav."

"Sam."

He had never really had to use his voice at his old school. All the students had been deaf, so everyone signed. Out in the wider world, Sam worried that he might not be saying the words right, and that this would make him stand out even more.

There was *one* place Sam never minded standing out. The moment he was on a football field, he felt as if he had come home. He wove across the field, ducking and diving as he drove the ball into the net again and again.

"Wow!" Rav said, after the game. "Can you be on our team all the time?"

Chapter 2

Silent Singing

Within a week of Sam starting at the new school, Dad had volunteered to help the older students with the kitchen garden. From out on the football field, Sam often saw Dad turning his face to lip-read as students asked him questions about planting herbs for cooking. It wasn't long until the summer holidays, and Dad was excited about helping them make treats for the end-of-term school concert.

Sam felt differently about the concert. He dreaded practising for it. Mr Wilson's class was performing a song, "Any Dream Will Do". Although Sam loved the vibrations from the instruments travelling through his body, he couldn't hear the melody. At first, he had tried to sing along, until a couple of girls had started giggling. From that moment, Sam tried only to whisper, and after a while he just mouthed the words instead.

At first, when everyone saw how good Sam was at sport, it seemed like they all wanted to be his friend. But now, singing with the class made him feel different and alone. Plus, he kept being left out. Groups of classmates seemed to suddenly leave the room. Or they were sent to do mysterious jobs at the office by Mr Wilson, without Sam ever being picked to join them.

Chapter 3

A Problem

"What's wrong?" Mum signed. They were meant to be celebrating her return. She had come back especially for the concert.

Sam shrugged, then signed, "Nothing."

Dad signed, "Mr Wilson says you're doing so well."

Sam blinked back tears. "I'm okay," he signed. He couldn't tell them about how much he hated practising for the concert. They had always said there was nothing wrong with him because he couldn't hear. He was different, but different was good. And unlike most kids, he spoke two languages, one with his mouth and the other with his hands.

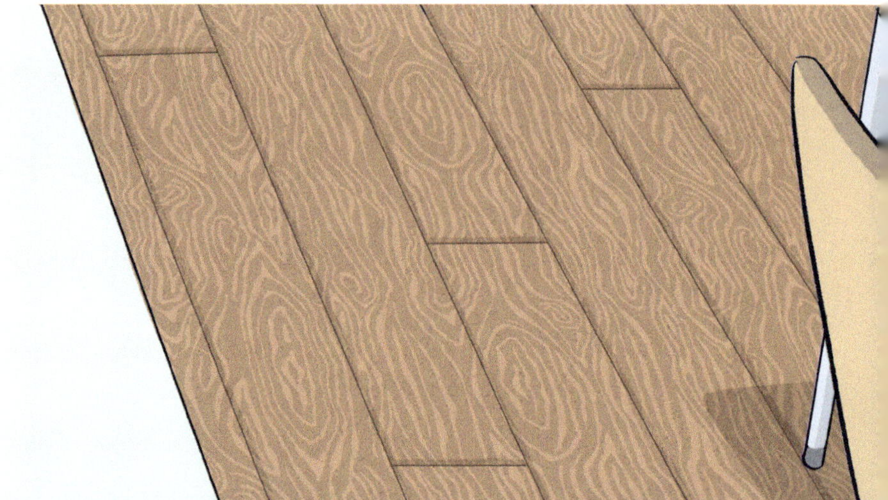

It was hard for Sam to complain when he knew that Dad had also been born deaf. But Dad hadn't let that stop him from travelling the world and winning prizes for his cooking.

How could Sam tell his parents how awful he felt, every time another group of kids was let out of class to help do a job? Or how the girls who had laughed at his singing had been made to apologise by Mr Wilson, and how embarrassed Sam had felt when he just wanted to blend in and fade into the shadows?

Chapter 4

Hiding

Sam could see Dad below, from where he was hiding.

Then Dad's head poked through the entrance to the treehouse. "We have to go," he signed. "We can't be late for the concert!"

"I'm not going," Sam signed.

"What is this really about?" signed Dad.

Sam blinked back tears as he signed, "I don't want to sing! I'm not strong or brave like you. I don't feel special. I hate being different."

To Sam's surprise, Dad didn't laugh. Instead, his face fell. "My lovely boy."

Sam was shocked to see a tear sliding down Dad's cheek. Dad reached out his arms and pulled Sam closer for a hug.

Dad gently pulled back to sign, "Deafness is a big part of who I am, and I have other talents, too. It will be the same for you."

Chapter 5

Any Dream Will Do

Sam shuffled onto the stage with the rest of his class. Through the hot blaze of the stage lights, he could see Mum's smiling face in the audience. Dad stood up the back with a small group of Year Six helpers.

The band started playing and the class sang.
Sam mouthed along.

When the song finished, Sam could hardly wait to race off the stage. But something strange was happening. The class remained standing. Mr Wilson told the audience, "And now we have a special surprise ..."

This time, the class sang "Any Dream Will Do", but Sam's classmates were singing by signing with their hands. Sam stared, then joined in – he knew all the words by heart.

At the back of the hall, Dad was also signing along with the song – and then Sam knew! All those "trips to the office" his classmates had made – they hadn't been going to the office at all. Dad had been teaching them how to sing "Any Dream Will Do" in sign language!

When the concert finished, Sam raced to the back of the hall. Before he was pulled away to play by his classmates, Sam hugged his father tight. His different dad was the best kind of dad in the world.